Full STEAM Ahead!

Math Matters

Subtraction in Action

I0809257

Adrianna Morganelli

CRABTREE
PUBLISHING COMPANY
WWW.CRABTREEBOOKS.COM

Title-Specific Learning Objectives:

Readers will:

- Describe subtraction as taking one number away from another, and identify subtraction clue words.
- Use visuals and clue words to complete subtraction problems.
- Identify the main ideas of the book and restate ideas in their own words.

High-frequency words (grade one)	Academic vocabulary
are, away, his, how, is, see, she, the	clue, coop, count, difference, minus, unit blocks

Before, During, and After Reading Prompts:

Activate Prior Knowledge and Make Predictions:
Have children read the title and look at the cover and title-page images. Ask children:

- What does "subtraction" mean? Have you subtracted before?
- How many chicks do you see on the title page? What is the difference between the number on the left and on the right?

During Reading:
After reading page 6, re-read clue words. Ask:

- Which words do you know? Which are new?
- Which words have been used in this book so far?

Tell children that they will be subtraction detectives when reading the rest of the book. Give each child one "clue" to look for. Have them write down the page number when they see and hear their clue mentioned.

After Reading:
Discuss the subtraction clues children found while reading the book. Make an anchor chart with all of the clues, with some child-created examples.

Pair children and have them use one of the clues to create a subtraction problem of their own, using objects around the classroom. Have each pair demonstrate by reading the problem and solving it.

Author: Adrianna Morganelli

Series Development: Reagan Miller

Editor: Janine Deschenes

Proofreader: Melissa Boyce

STEAM Notes for Educators: Reagan Miller and Janine Deschenes

Guided Reading Leveling: Publishing Solutions Group

Cover, Interior Design, and Prepress: Samara Parent

Photo research: Janine Deschenes and Samara Parent

Production coordinator: Katherine Berti

Photographs:
iStock: Topalov: front cover; martinedoucet: p. 4, p. 8; Kemter: p. 16
Shutterstock: Phil's Mommy: p. 18 (all), p. 19 (all)), p. 20 (all), p. 21 (bottom)
All other photographs by Shutterstock

Library and Archives Canada Cataloguing in Publication

Morganelli, Adrianna, 1979-, author
Subtraction in action / Adrianna Morganelli.

(Full STEAM ahead!)
Includes index.
Issued in print and electronic formats.
ISBN 978-0-7787-6233-1 (hardcover).--
ISBN 978-0-7787-6311-6 (softcover).--ISBN 978-1-4271-2272-8 (HTML)

1. Subtraction--Juvenile literature. I. Title.

QA115.M67 2019 j513.2'12 C2018-906235-5
C2018-906236-3

Library of Congress Cataloging-in-Publication Data

Names: Morganelli, Adrianna, 1979- author.
Title: Subtraction in action / Adrianna Morganelli.
Description: New York, New York : Crabtree Publishing Company, [2019] | Series: Full STEAM ahead! | Includes index.
Identifiers: LCCN 2018056804 (print) | LCCN 2019003086 (ebook) | ISBN 9781427122728 (Electronic) | ISBN 9780778762331 (hardcover : alk. paper) | ISBN 9780778763116 (pbk. : alk. paper)
Subjects: LCSH: Subtraction--Juvenile literature. | Arithmetic--Juvenile literature.
Classification: LCC QA115 (ebook) | LCC QA115 .M725 2019 (print) | DDC 513.2/12--dc23
LC record available at https://lccn.loc.gov/2018056804

Printed in the U.S.A./042019/CG20190215

Table of Contents

Crabtree Publishing Company
www.crabtreebooks.com 1-800-387-7650

In Canada: We acknowledge the financial support of the Government of Canada through the Book Publishing Industry Development Program (BPIDP) for our publishing activities.

Published in Canada
Crabtree Publishing
616 Welland Ave.
St. Catharines, Ontario
L2M 5V6

Published in the United States
Crabtree Publishing
PMB 59051
350 Fifth Avenue, 59th Floor
New York, New York 10118

Published in the United Kingdom
Crabtree Publishing
Maritime House
Basin Road North, Hove
BN41 1WR

Published in Australia
Crabtree Publishing
Unit 3 – 5 Currumbin Court
Capalaba
QLD 4157

Missing Chickens

Leo loves to visit his uncle's farm. Today Leo's friend Angelica is visiting the farm too!

Leo shows Angelica around the farm.

There are ten chickens on the farm.
Leo takes Angelica to the chicken coop.
She **counts** the chickens. She only sees six.

Angelica wonders how many chickens are missing.

Time to Subtract

The friends can use **subtraction** to find the number of missing chickens. Subtraction is taking one number away from another.

Subtraction Clues
These words tell us to subtract.

How many left?

What is the **difference**?

Take away

How many more?

Minus

How many less?

Angelica and Leo need to take six away from ten.
"Take away" is a **clue** to use subtraction.

There are ten chickens in all. Angelica saw six. Take six away from ten. How many are left?

Ten minus six is four. There are four chickens missing.

How Many Left?

In the morning, Leo helped his uncle **collect** eggs. Leo shows Angelica the eggs. "Wow! How many eggs are there?" she asks.

Leo and Angelica count the eggs. There are 20.

Oh no! Five eggs fell out of the basket. Leo wonders how many eggs are left. Subtraction will tell us how many eggs are left after some are taken away.

20 – 5 = 15

There are 15 eggs left in the basket.

Solve a Pig Problem

Leo shows Angelica the pigpen. The friends count seven pigs. Some of the pigs roll in the mud to keep cool. They count four pigs in the mud.

Angelica and Leo want to know how many pigs are not in the mud. Can you help them find the number?

Take four pigs away from seven. What is the difference? How many pigs are not in the mud?

Subtract with Zero

A number minus the same number equals zero. Three cows lie in the grass. Three cows fall asleep. How many cows are awake? Zero!

Three minus three equals zero.

When zero is subtracted from a number, the number stays the same.

There are five kittens playing in the barn. Five have orange fur. None have black fur. How many kittens have orange fur?

How Many More?

Leo and Angelica picked apples after lunch. Leo picked 10 baskets of apples.

Angelica picked 12 baskets of apples. How many more baskets did Angelica pick?

Subtract the smaller number from the larger number: 12 – 10 = 2. Angelica picked 2 more baskets of apples.

Subtract the Crows

Leo's uncle has two scarecrows.

The crows do not think the scarecrows are very scary! They fly to the scarecrows.

The short scarecrow has eight crows.
The tall scarecrow has three crows.

$$8 - 3 = ?$$

How many more crows fly to the short scarecrow?

Subtract with Blocks

Leo and Angelica bring some apples to school the next day. At school they use **unit blocks** to help them subtract.

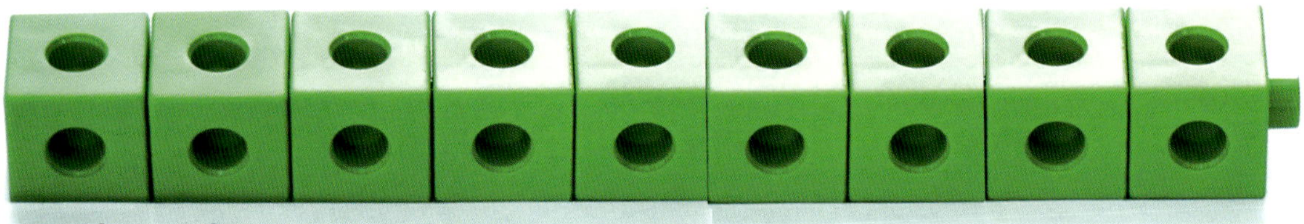

Leo brought nine apples.

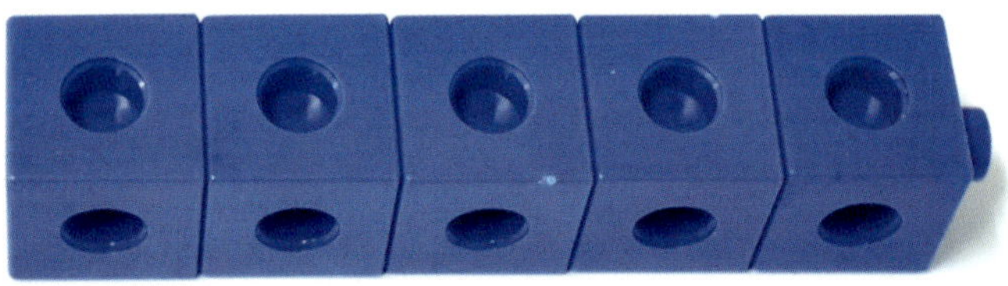

Angelica brought five apples.

9 – 5 = ?

How many less did Angelica bring?

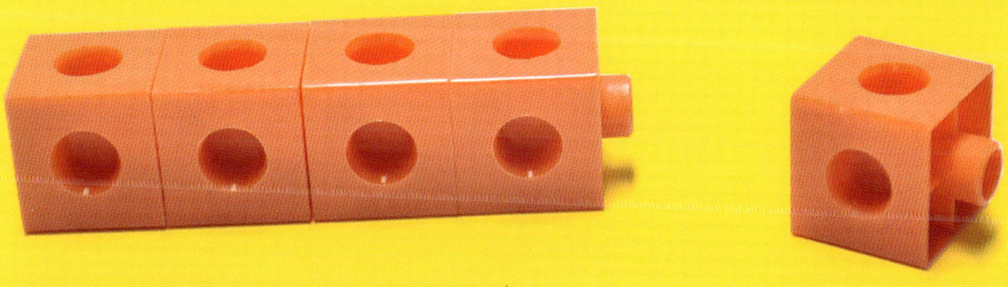

5 – 1 = ?

Angelica eats one of her apples. Take one away from five.
How many apples does she have left?

9 – 6 = ?

Leo shares his apples with Katie, Dylan, and Amin.
They eat six apples. How many apples does Leo have left?

Practice, Practice!

Angelica, Leo, and their friends practice subtraction with unit blocks. Can you help them find the answers?

6 – 3 = ?

Take three away from six. How many are left?

5 – 4 = ?

What is five minus four?

12 – 8 = ?

What is the difference between twelve and eight?

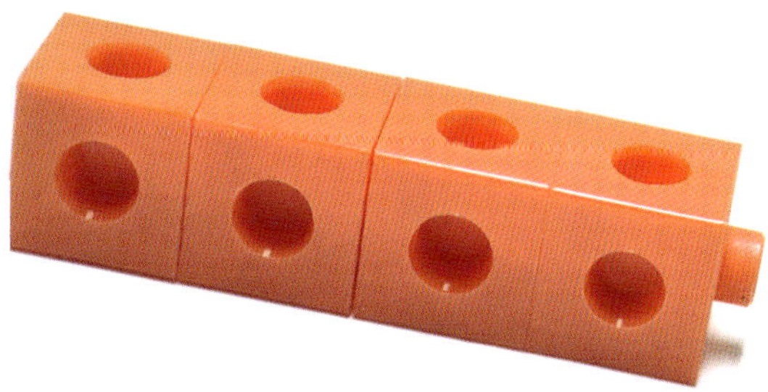

9 – 4 = ?

How many more blue blocks than red blocks?

Words to Know

clue [kloo] noun
Something that helps a person find something or solve a problem

collect [kuh-LEKT] verb
To gather together objects from different places, often to create a collection or larger group

counts [kounts] verb
Adds to find the total number of objects in a group

difference [DIF-er-uhns] noun The number that is left when a smaller number is subtracted from a larger number

subtraction [suh b-TRAK-shuh n] noun Taking one number away from another

unit blocks [YOO-nit bloks] noun Single blocks that take the place of numbers

A noun is a person, place, or thing.

A verb is an action word that tells you what someone or something does.

An adjective is a word that tells you what something is like.

Index

About the Author

Adrianna Morganelli is an editor and writer who has worked with Crabtree Publishing on countless book titles. She is currently working on a children's novel.

To explore and learn more, enter the code at the Crabtree Plus website below.

www.crabtreeplus.com/fullsteamahead

Your code is:
fsa20

STEAM Notes for Educators

Full STEAM Ahead is a literacy series that helps readers build vocabulary, fluency, and comprehension while learning about big ideas in STEAM subjects. *Subtraction in Action* explains and repeats subtraction clues to help readers identify and solve subtraction problems. The STEAM activity below helps readers extend the ideas in the book to build their skills in math, arts, and language arts.

Creating a Subtraction Story

Children will be able to:

- Create and solve subtraction problems.
- Create an illustrated story that involves a subtraction problem.

Materials

- Subtraction Story Planning Sheet
- Subtraction Story Template
- Subtraction Story Completed Example
- Art tools for illustrations, such as crayons

Guiding Prompts

After reading *Subtraction in Action*, ask children:

- How does the book help us learn to subtract? Review some examples and practice.
- Can you think of your own subtraction question? Use classroom objects to demonstrate and ask children to share ideas.
- How does the story of Leo and Angelica help make learning about subtraction fun?

Activity Prompts

Explain to children that they will demonstrate their new subtraction knowledge by creating a fun, illustrated story about a subtraction problem! Remind them that stories can help make learning about math fun.

Children can work in pairs. Show them the Subtraction Story Completed Example and hand each pair a Planning Sheet. Their stories must include:

- A subtraction problem
- At least one subtraction clue word (review words on page 6)
- At least two characters
- A minimum of eight sentences
- Four or more illustrations

Check with children as they plan their story to ensure they are on the right track. When their plan meets the criteria, they can create a good copy on the Subtraction Story Template.

Have children present their stories to their peers.

- Listeners should participate by identifying or solving the subtraction problem in the story.

Extensions

- Have children act out their subtraction story. They can act the roles, or use puppets.

To view and download the worksheets, visit **www.crabtreebooks.com/resources/printables** or **www.crabtreeplus.com/fullsteamahead** and enter the code **fsa20**.